GIRLHOOD Journeys

Marie

An Invitation to Dance
France, 1775

by Kathleen V. Kudlinski

illustrated by
Lyn Durham

GIRLHOOD JOURNEYS COLLECTION®

ALADDIN PAPERBACKS

Grateful acknowledgement is made to Giraudon/Art Resource, NY for the use of the illustrations on pages 68 and 70, both from the Musée de la Ville de Paris, Musée Carnavalet, Paris, France

First Aladdin Paperbacks edition October 1996
Copyright © 1996 by Girlhood Journeys, Inc.

Aladdin Paperbacks
An imprint of Simon & Schuster
Children's Publishing Division
1230 Avenue of the Americas
New York, NY 10020

Designed by Wendy Letven Design
The text of this book is set in Garamond.

10 9 8 7 6 5 4 3

Also available in a Simon & Schuster Books for Young Readers
hardcover edition.

The Library of Congress has cataloged the hardcover edition
as follows:
Kudlinski, Kathleen V.
Marie: an invitation to dance, France 1775 / by Kathleen V. Kudlinski;
illustrated by Lyn Durham.
p. cm. — (Girlhood journeys)
"Girlhood Journeys Collection."
Summary: Ten-year-old Marie dreams of becoming a ballerina, but without
a wealthy sponsor, she faces a more mundane future dictated by her family's
position in pre-Revolutionary Parisian society.
ISBN 0-689-81139-X
[1. Ballet—Fiction. 2. Paris (France)—Fiction.] I. Durham, Lyn, ill. II.
Title. III. Series.
PZ7.K9486Mar   1996
[Fic]—dc20   96-15062

ISBN 0-689-80985-9 (Aladdin pbk.)

Reprinted by arrangement with Aladdin Paperbacks,
an imprint of Simon & Schuster Children's Publishing Division.

C O N T E N T S

For Betsy, my daughter,
whose heart dances
when she is on horseback.

How to Say Marie's French Words

Ballet
(bal-AY)

Bonjour
(bohn-SZURE) good day
(or hello)

C'est la vie
(seh-la-vee) that is life

Café
(caff-AY) coffee or a place where
coffee is served

Chocolat
(SHOK-o-lah) chocolate or
hot cocoa

Croissant
(cwah-SAHN) a crescent-
shaped roll

Éclair
(eh-CLARE) a pudding-filled
pastry with chocolate icing

Gabrielle
(gah-bree-EL) a girl's name

Joelle
(szhoe-EL) a girl's name,
meaning joy

Ma chérie
(ma sherr-REE) my friend
(if it is a girl friend);
a friend who is a boy
is called "mon cher"
(mohn-SHER)

Madame
(ma-DAHM)
Missus or Mrs., a married lady

Mademoiselle
(mad-mwa-szell)
Miss, an unmarried lady

Maman
(ma-MAHN)
Mom

Marie
(mah-RHEE)
a girl's name

Merci
(mare-SEE)
thank you

Mon Dieu
(mon-DIEU)
an exclamation;
literally My God

Monsieur
(miss-SIEUR)
Mister or Mr.

Non
(nohn) no

Oui
(wee) yes

Pas de chat
(pah-duh-SHA)
a ballet step,
literally step of the cat

Papa
(pa-PAH) Dad

Sou
(soo) a French coin

CHAPTER ONE

FOOTSTEPS

M arie felt hands close tightly over her eyes. The warm Paris sunshine disappeared, and the smell of fresh bread floated in the air.

"Is it my best of friends?" Marie guessed. The hands moved, and Joelle swirled around, skirts and apron fluttering, and flopped onto the park bench beside Marie.

"How do you always know it's me?" she complained.

"I know your footsteps."

"You do?"

Marie nodded. "*Oui.* I always listen to people's walks. Don't you?"

"*Non.*" Joelle looked down at her feet. "You can't really tell people by their steps, can you?"

Marie stood up. "Listen. This is you,

walking." She let her feet roll to the sides. "Your papa limps a little on his right foot." Marie took a few more steps. The limp hardly showed, but it changed the sound. Joelle nodded, her eyes wide.

"That's Papa exactly!" she said.

"Your *maman* walks hard on her heels, like she is tired and angry." Marie paced past the bench. "Mine steps softly." Her movements changed only a little, but her footsteps sounded very different. "Her steps are hurried, but careful. My little sister Anne walks like any five-year-old." Marie's shoes tapped lightly on the cobblestones.

"Show me someone else!" Joelle demanded.

"Here is a lady from court." Marie pulled herself up tall and took tiny, mincing steps. She kept her head exactly level. "King Louis, Queen Marie Antoinette, all the duchesses," she said, "even the ladies-in-waiting; they all walk like this."

Joelle clapped her hands. "You're right! They always look like they're gliding. From under your skirts, though, your steps sound like a child's!"

"These little steps should be taking me home, Joelle," Marie said with a sigh. "Maman will be needing me in the *café.*"

"Oh!" Joelle leaped to her feet. "I was

supposed to be back at the pastry shop. Where did the time go?"

The friends walked hand in hand through the Paris streets. *"Bonjour,"* Joelle greeted passing nuns with a nod. She waved to children playing in the mud and curtsied to strange young men. Marie helped to steady Joelle as they jumped over smelly gutters and wide puddles.

"Look out!" she cried once, pulling Joelle out of the way as an elegant carriage clattered past. The noise of hoofbeats and iron-edged wheels on cobblestones echoed between the tall apartment buildings.

"Bonjour," Joelle said to a policeman. He smiled and nodded to her. Joelle turned to her friend. "Why don't you talk to people on the street?"

Marie thought a moment. "I suppose I am too shy," she said quietly.

"You? Shy?" Joelle laughed. "You would dance in front of the queen herself!"

"That is different." Marie tried to explain. "I would rather dance than anything else in the world. It is far better than talking. What if I say the wrong thing to the wrong person? Or someone doesn't understand what I mean? Or

gets angry?" *What if they don't like me*, she added to herself. "When I am dancing, I am an actor on a stage. I am not myself."

Joelle shook her head and smiled. "You are always Marie, and I am lucky to be your friend." They walked on. "Bonjour," she greeted a flower girl. "Your violets are so beautiful today!" The street vendor nodded her thanks and handed Joelle a perfect lavender flower.

"You are amazing." Marie shook her head.

"You talk all day long to strangers at your maman's café."

"But that is my job," Marie explained. "And now I am late." The two friends said a hurried good-bye. Joelle ducked into the door of her father's pastry shop. Marie rushed next door to the Café La Marche.

"Bonjour, Marie!" customers called from many tables.

"Good morning, my friends," she called in return, and went to work.❖

CHAPTER TWO

NEWS

Marie hurried to the breakfast table the next morning. She stopped to kiss Papa on the cheek and to brush his shoulder clean. "Powder from your wig, Papa," she explained, sitting down. "Is that a new wig? Does that mean you are off on another business trip?"

"Oui," Papa said. "Today I am traveling to Versailles."

"Oh, Papa!" Marie knew she shouldn't interrupt, but she couldn't help herself. "To the palace? Will you see the new queen?" She pictured the beautiful Marie Antoinette in one of her famous gowns. All of Paris was talking about her. "Will you see the dancers at court?"

"Hush, Marie. Too many questions. At ten, you should be more careful with your words," Maman said. "Remember your etiquette, *ma chérie.*"

Marie quietly unfolded her napkin and placed it across her skirts. *"Merci,"* she told the maid who handed her a hot *chocolat* in a tiny china cup. And she said "thank you" again when she was given a saucer of milk and a piece of bread to break into it. She and her sisters and the servants listened silently as her parents discussed the day.

"I shall be gone only a night," Papa was saying. "I've got lace and china to trade, but there simply is no grain or flour." Marie heard one of the maids sigh.

And there was more news. "Be sure everything is ready for the new boarders," Papa told Maman. "They should arrive before noon."

"Marie will see to their rooms," Maman said, looking at her daughter. Marie nodded. New boarders? The old ballerina, *Madame* Gabrielle, had been their only guest for so long, Marie had almost forgotten there was room for more people.

She leaned forward in her chair, but Papa and Maman said nothing else about the new people or Papa's business at the palace.

"Who is coming to live with us now?" Marie asked Maman as they opened the doors of the Café La Marche.

"An artist and his daughter. *Monsieur* and *Mademoiselle* Williams." Marie looked at her quickly. "Non, dear," Maman answered the question in Marie's eyes. "Gabrielle may be teaching you ballet, but we can't ask Monsieur Williams to give you art lessons."

She shook the crumbs out of a tablecloth, and Marie helped her spread it back on the table. "They arrive this morning," Maman went on. "The mademoiselle will be studying painting here. She is older than you, just thirteen."

"She is almost old enough to be married." Marie could not keep the dread out of her voice.

"You're not too young to begin thinking about it yourself, Marie. Your papa has already begun to look for a husband for you." Maman smiled at her daughter. Marie did not smile back. *I want to dance,* she thought, *before I have to marry. Or run a house. Or have babies.* She sighed.

"Perhaps late marriages are the custom in British colonies," Maman went on. "And who is to judge?"

"They're British?" Marie was horrified. "We are renting our rooms to an Englishman?"

"Non. The Williamses are from New Haven in the Connecticut colony. In America." Marie stood, stunned. "You can close your mouth now, Marie," Maman teased. "You look a bit like a fish. Go and see that the rooms are ready. I have to talk to Cook about today's meals."

"Marie?" Joelle came through the café door.

"Oh, bonjour, ma chérie," Marie greeted her best friend with a hug. "I have such news to share. You'll never guess who is coming to stay!"

"You have new boarders?" Joelle asked.

"From the American colonies!" Marie told her. "Here! Can you imagine?"

Joelle followed her upstairs into the empty rooms, asking a question with every breath. "Do they speak French? Who are they? Is it a family? Is there another girl? Why are they in Paris?"

Marie told her everything she knew as she opened the window to let light and fresh air into the rooms. Together, they pulled the bed drapes back to air the bedchambers. "I think I'll set out a dish of potpourri," Marie said. "The scent of herbs

and dry flowers will help clear out the stale air."

"A vase of fresh flowers would be pretty, too," Joelle said.

"We'll get some," Marie agreed. She checked the chamber pots under the beds and the water pitchers in the washstands. All were clean and in order. "Let's leave a few sweet cakes from your papa's shop on their bed tables, too," she said.

"Do American girls wear wigs or caps?" Marie wondered out loud, looking at the ruffled cap covering Joelle's dark curls. "Do they wear corsets like we do? Can they do a proper curtsy?" Joelle shrugged. "The college students who come to the café call Americans noble savages," Marie went on. "You don't suppose they wear leather moccasins, do you?"

"Savages? Here?" Joelle looked around the elegant cream and white room. Marie pretended to do a savage native dance on the flowered carpet, and they both laughed.

The best friends ran next door to the pastry shop. "Joelle!" Monsieur Du Pont called through the open door. "An *éclair* for you and one for Marie?"

Joelle answered, "Oui, Papa, and we'll need two more for the La Marches' new boarders."

Marie thought about the rich chocolaty icing and creamy pudding inside, but shook her head. "None for me, thank you, Monsieur." She turned to Joelle. "You know what Madame Gabrielle says, 'You can dance lightly . . .'"

" '. . . or,' " Joelle finished with her, " 'you can eat sweets.' Well, Marie, I have no need to dance, but I do seem to need sweets!" She giggled and bit into the éclair.

"You'd best have your treat inside the shop today," Joelle's papa said.

"Why can't I eat it while we walk to the market?" Joelle licked the dark brown icing off her fingers. Marie tried not to watch.

"There's been no flour delivered today," Monsieur Du Pont explained, "and many in the city are going without bread."

Marie looked at the last of the éclair and remembered the one slice of bread she'd had for breakfast. "Why is there no flour?" she asked Monsieur Du Pont.

"Our fine king's taxes and laws," he grumbled.

Marie wanted to ask more questions, but Joelle was pulling at her hand. "None of this matters to us," she said. "Let's go buy some flowers for your rooms."

They walked past a row of book stands and a juggler, a fruit seller singing her song, and a puppet theater. University students walked by in little knots, waving their arms and arguing in Latin. "*Ave*, Marie," one said.

"Ave, Henri," she answered her friend from the café. The girls strolled past nuns picking the season's first weeds in the warm sun of the convent garden. Children played and dodged the carriages that rushed through the narrow streets. Everyone stepped carefully over the slime in the gutters.

"Shall we get red and yellow tulips for the 'savages' or these deep blue iris?" Joelle stood in front of a booth filled with fresh spring flowers.

"The iris, of course," Marie said. "Fleur-de-lis to welcome our guests to France."

On the way home, the girls stopped on a corner to watch a street dancer dressed as a Harlequin. His face was painted half black and half white, a mask hid his eyes, and he wore a tight suit in a colorful, diamond-shaped pattern. Marie could stand still for only a moment before she started swaying in time with the dancer. Then her feet began to mimic his steps. The Harlequin bowed to her.

"Go ahead," Joelle whispered. Marie curtsied and took the Harlequin's hand. She knew his dance; it was the minuet that Gabrielle had taught her. As they danced, the Harlequin began moving faster, and Marie picked up her pace to match his. Around them, people stopped to watch and began laughing. An elegant carriage pulled to a halt in the street, and a fine lady stepped out to watch, holding her satin skirts up out of the mud. Still, Marie danced.

She could feel her face flush and her hair come loose. Her corset pinched her ribs, but it was so delicious to dance with a real partner that none of that mattered. Faster and faster they danced. The Harlequin was the first to miss a step and trip.

Finally he stopped and bowed to her, panting, while the crowd clapped. The aristocratic stranger was starting to glide toward them when a church bell chimed across the river. Marie gasped. "Joelle, the Americans! We must hurry!"

They rushed home, but before she entered the café, Marie paused to smooth her hair into place. She took a few slow breaths, straightened her shoulders, shook the dust from her skirts, and checked to see that no mud clung to her shoes.

"Who was that beautiful lady?" Joelle asked her. "Did you see her gown?" Marie looked at Joelle's dress, limp and dusted with flour as always. "Was she a messenger from court?" Joelle wondered. "A duchess, a countess?"

Marie shrugged her shoulders, but she couldn't help wondering, too. The woman's sharp green eyes had followed every step of her dance.❖

SAVAGES

J oelle arranged the iris in a vase while Marie measured out dried rose petals and lilac blossoms into a dish. "Shall I add rosemary or mint to the potpourri?" she asked.

"Oh, why not use both?" Joelle said. "But throw in some tansy to keep away the flies. And hurry."

The girls were just putting their finishing touches onto the room when they heard footsteps on the stairs. "Follow me," Maman was saying.

Marie froze. Their guests were here! "Quick, Joelle," she said. "Straighten your cap." The girls stood side by side as the Americans came through the door. *He is so tall,* Marie thought, *and she is so pretty!* She only had a moment to see a beautiful pink gown with rosebuds at the waist and a dainty white cap perched on pale yellow hair before Maman began introducing the new boarders.

"Monsieur Williams, this is my daughter, Marie, and her friend Joelle." Maman looked surprised at seeing the girls there, but she kept her voice steady. Marie swept into a deep curtsy, and Joelle followed. As they rose gracefully, Monseiur Williams spoke.

"May I introduce my daughter, Prudence." Marie dipped again in greeting, but not before she saw that Prudence's curtsy was just as deep and steady as her own. Beside her, Joelle struggled back to her feet.

"Bonjour, Mademoiselles," Prudence said. "I hope we can explore Paris together this spring."

"Your French is excellent," Marie complimented her. In truth, the American spoke with a strange accent.

"Oh, non, I am only a beginner," Prudence protested. "With your help, I will learn more of your lovely language." Marie smiled into Prudence's blue eyes. *This is no savage,* she thought. *Even Maman herself could find no fault with her etiquette.*

"Here's the last of it." A carriage driver set two wooden suitcases onto a pile of trunks on the carpet.

"My paints!" Prudence said. "I haven't seen them since we left home, two months ago." She pulled off a glove, opened a box, and stroked a paintbrush. Marie tried to imagine how it would feel not to dance for two months.

"We could take you to a lovely spot to paint this afternoon," she said.

"You are so very thoughtful," Prudence said. "Papa, may I start to work at once?"

"As soon as we are unpacked, my dear."

"When you are ready to paint, I will be downstairs in the café," Marie told Prudence.

"Oh, Marie," said Joelle as the girls made their way downstairs. "Did you see her dress? It looks like it came straight from a Paris dress shop. Is that how the colonials all look?" Joelle straightened the white scarf that made a collar on her old everyday dress.

"Her outfit is a year or so behind the fanciest styles," Marie said thoughtfully, "but isn't she a lovely person?"

"She sounds funny when she talks," Joelle said. "Where are you taking her to paint?"

"Don't you want to come along?" Marie asked.

"Only if I won't be in the way," Joelle said. Marie glanced at her quickly. Joelle would not look in her eyes.

"Oh, Joelle, you will always be my first and dearest friend." Marie hugged her. "Now I have to get to work. We will come by to get you when Mademoiselle Prudence is ready to go painting."

• • •

"Bonjour, Marie!" The friendly calls began as soon as she entered the café. "Sit here, Mademoiselle." "No, come sit with us."

Marie smiled and poured herself a cup that was half coffee and half milk. "Bring me a *café au lait,* too, Mademoiselle!" Maman had serving maids to fetch and carry for the customers, but they liked to be waited on by the hostesses, who had time to sit and talk with them.

"Ave, Marie! Come visit us!"

"Ave!" Marie called back to a black-robed student. She liked learning the Latin that everyone at the universities spoke.

"And who is the mysterious new beauty at the Hôtel La Marche?" one of them asked.

Marie stirred a tiny spoon of sugar into her cup. *Tell one student and they'll all know,* she reminded herself. These young men gossiped worse than any women. There couldn't be any harm in knowing a name, she decided. "She is Prudence Williams, from the Connecticut colony in America."

"Ah, an American." They all were interested. "She is here to avoid the war, then."

What war? Marie wanted to ask. Instead she listened. "The colonials are brave to try to break free from the king of England," one student said.

"Oh, they'll just set up another king in his place. A country can't survive without a king," an older man said from the next table. Marie noticed the fur edges on his gown. *A professor,* she thought.

"Only a fool would want to live under King George," someone said. Everybody nodded.

"Any defeat for the king of England is a victory for France!" One student raised his wineglass, and the rest all followed.

"Ah, but some say a defeat of our own king would be a victory for Frenchmen."

Suddenly there was silence. Marie bit her lip. How could she change the subject? She thought fast. "Our good Prudence has come to make paintings, not war," she said.

"Oh, so she's an art student! Another painter like you, Henri."

"But she is much prettier than you!" And once again the students were laughing and teasing. Marie moved to another table.

"Does little Joelle's papa have grain to grind into flour?" another professor asked her.

"I suppose so," Marie said. "Did you want a pastry with that chocolat?" She rose to go next door.

"Oh, non, non," the man said. "But Monsieur Du Pont is one of the lucky ones."

"He is for now," another teacher at the table said. "But if a man's children are hungry enough, he will take what he needs by force. These are dangerous times." Marie did not like the talk at this table, either. How could she change it?

"It is the springtime," she agreed. "And we are all in danger of falling in love in spring."

"And what would you know of that, wee Mademoiselle?" the professor teased. Marie could feel her face flush as all the men laughed. She was tired of trying to keep the conversation light and happy. How did Maman do this all day, she wondered. Her shoulders felt stiff. She couldn't wait for today's ballet lesson in Madame Gabrielle's room. Marie moved to the next table.

"Bonjour, Marie!" a writer said. "What do you think of our good king?" *I think Louis is a good king,* she wanted to say. *And Marie Antoinette would be a fine queen, if only you would give her a chance. Take care with your words,* she reminded herself, and bit her lip instead of answering.

"Marie?" Prudence was standing at the café door with her paint box and a parasol. All the students stopped talking to look at her.

"Oh, Prudence, I am so glad to see you!" Marie said.

"Why, thank you," the American girl said. "Can you leave soon to show me that pretty scene in Paris?"

"Now," Marie said quickly. "I think I can leave now." At a nod from her *maman*, Marie hurried out the door.

"Is there something wrong?" Prudence asked out on the street.

"There is so much trouble right now." Marie shook her head, thinking of the flour shortage, hungry children, and so many angry men. "It worries me," she said.

"That is how it is on the streets of New Haven, too. Sometimes at home I am very frightened."

Marie looked at the older girl. Her blue eyes looked sympathetic. "What do you do when you are worried?" Marie asked.

"I paint," Prudence said, simply. "And then I forget everything else."

Marie thought a moment, nodded, then said, "When I dance, nothing else matters."

"You must show me," Prudence said. "I love the dance."

"Is it time to go and paint?" Joelle stepped out of the pastry shop as they passed.

"Oui. Joelle, what do you do when you are

worried?" Marie asked as they walked toward the
river.

"I never bother worrying." Joelle smiled.
"What's the use?"

"But all of Paris seems to be upset about one
thing or another," Marie said.

"C'est la vie." Joelle shrugged.

"Say-la-vee?" Prudence repeated. "What does
that mean?"

"It means, 'That is life.' I say it a lot, don't I,
Marie? Things are just the way they are, and I
can't change them."

"Oh, *Mon Dieu!*" Prudence stopped still as
they turned a corner. "How beautiful!" Before
them, barges floated in the Seine River. Beyond
the river, the huge cathedral of Notre-Dame soared
against the sky. Afternoon sun lit the tall spires
and sparkled against the stained-glass windows.
"Marie, you were right. I must paint this."

"Let's get out of the road, first," Joelle suggested.

Prudence laughed. "Of course." As she set up
her easel, Marie gazed up at the cathedral. She
passed this way often, but she hadn't stopped to
look—really look—at the cathedral in months. The
light picked out every carving on the stone building,
from the gentle saints who stood above the doors to

the ugly gargoyles sprouting
from the corners of the roof.
They'd all stood in their
places for hundreds of years,
Marie thought, no matter
what the people were saying
on the streets below.

Prudence began to
sketch, and Marie thought
of other places that would make beautiful
paintings. "Will you be working every day?" she
asked hopefully. Paris looked different, she
thought, when you were standing beside an artist.

"What?" Prudence sketched in Notre-Dame's
twin towers. "Ah, will I be working every day?"
She changed a line. "Ah, yes." She drew the
cathedral's graceful stone pillars. "Every day that I,
um, can." Marie decided not to interrupt again.
Prudence really did seem to forget everything
when she painted. Marie sat on a sunbaked stone
bench with Joelle and watched Notre-Dame
appear, bit by bit, on Prudence's drawing pad. The
sun warmed her skin through her dress, the river
murmured at her feet, and the cathedral bells
began to ring. She might be sitting very still,
Marie thought, but inside, she was dancing. ❖

THE DANCE

"Count to yourself, now, Marie," Gabrielle said. She stopped tapping her fan against the windowsill. Marie tried to keep the beat in her head and remember the steps at the same time. *Pirouette and leap and step and together,* she chanted silently, *pas de chat, pas de chat, pas de chat.* She loved the three steps of the cat that ended the series. Marie finished the set

and brought her body back to graceful stillness.

"Round your arms," Gabrielle scolded, "stretch your neck, drop your shoulders, and start again at the beginning." Marie smiled. *Nothing is ever good enough for Gabrielle,* she thought. "Remember, keep your eyes on one thing as you turn," Madame was saying. "That way you won't lose your balance." *The harder I try, the more I learn,* Marie reminded herself. She practiced a quick pirouette, keeping her eyes on one spot.

She pushed a long curl back into place and looked at Gabrielle's hair. It was as white as a wig, and every hair was perfect. "How do ballerinas onstage at the opera keep their hair up?"

"They all wear very stiff wigs, Marie. Their faces are stiff with makeup, too!"

"Do you keep special dresses for them?" Marie wished she could see an opera performance from backstage, the way Gabrielle did every night. Her parents would not let her go alone, and Papa did not have time for the opera.

"Oui. Dancers' skirts are so short that their ankles show," Gabrielle said.

Marie gasped. No wonder every step had to be just right! Marie practiced the dance set again, pretending there were no skirts to swish against her shoe buckles.

Three quick knocks sounded at the door. "Madame?" It was Prudence's voice. "May I come in?"

Gabrielle turned to Marie. "Do you mind stopping your lesson for a moment?" In answer, Marie opened the door.

Prudence hurried in, then stopped, suddenly. "I'm so sorry, Madame and Mademoiselle." She curtsied deeply. "It was silent beyond the door. I forgot about Marie's lesson."

"Teaching Marie is a joy," Gabrielle said. Marie looked at the floor. It was strange to be talked about, but wonderful to hear what Madame had to say. "She has exceptional talent as a dancer," Gabrielle went on. "Marie could be one of the greatest of dancers, if only . . ."

"She would need a sponsor from court?" Prudence asked. "Someone very rich?"

"From what my old friends at court tell me, Marie already dances well enough to pass as a ballerina," Gabrielle said. Marie could not believe she was hearing this. "But she needs more training than I can give her, and that is very expensive. Without a sponsor . . ."

Marie tried to make her voice sound bright. "C'est la vie." She turned to Prudence. "Do the Americans have any new dance steps that I could learn?"

"I can show you a reel," Prudence said. "This is the Virginia reel. The dance needs more people, but we can pretend." She gathered her skirts in her hands, raised them to her ankles, curtsied, and began a quick series of fancy steps. By the time Gabrielle and Marie had learned the steps, all three were laughing and breathless.

"Oh, Madame, I nearly forgot what I came for." Prudence turned at the door. "Could you arrange to get tickets for Papa and me for opening night at the Opéra next week?"

Gabrielle looked surprised, then she nodded slowly. "On one condition," she said. "You must take Marie along. She should see her dream."

Please, Marie wanted to beg. *Neither Maman nor Papa has the time to take me. Please take me.*

Prudence looked at her face and smiled. "My papa brought me here to follow my dream," she said. "I am sure he will agree to take Marie and her friend Joelle, too, to the Opéra. Does the Mademoiselle in question wish to come with us?"

Marie answered with a grand curtsy.

"Oh, Madame, thank you!" Marie said as the door closed.

Gabrielle eased herself into a seat by her

writing desk and began sharpening a feather quill. "Is my lesson over?" Marie asked. Madame's old injury seemed to be hurting more than usual, Marie thought.

"Oui." Madame dipped the quill pen into an ink bottle and began writing on a sheet of cream-colored paper. "I think all of us have danced enough for one day, don't you?"

"I shall see you tomorrow, then?" Marie said.

Without looking up, Gabrielle nodded. "Oui."

Marie hurried to her own room, smiling at the wonderful secrets she'd heard. Madame had said she could be a great dancer. And in one week she would be watching the ballet dancers at the Paris Opéra! She poured water from the pitcher into her washbasin and splashed her sweaty face. Reaching for the towel, she began to sway and to dance the new steps of the Virginia reel.

As she danced, the last of her upswept curls fell. Marie looked in the mirror, sighed, and pulled all the ribbons and pins out so her long hair could swing free. *Someday,* she promised herself, making a wild pirouette, *someday I will dance on a real stage.*

She imagined the music of a real orchestra and practiced the steps Gabrielle had taught her one last time, making sure each move was absolutely perfect. Then she curtsied grandly to her make-believe audience and laughed out loud.❖

TEARS

"Hush," the nursemaid scolded Marie's sisters. Maman gave a warning glance down the table at them, but the little ones kept fussing. "Why can't I have croissants with my chocolat?" Anne whined.

"I want a sweet roll, not a custard!" four-year-old Thérèse said, knocking over her cup. A serving girl hurried to wipe up the chocolat spreading across the tablecloth.

"Enough," Papa finally said. "I will have my breakfast in peace. Nurse, take them away."

"Beg pardon, Monsieur," she apologized. She tried to get three cranky little girls to leave the table quietly. It didn't work.

"Why do we have to go?" Thérèse whined. Hélène, the youngest, started crying.

"Help her, Marie."

But I work in the café now, she wanted to say. *I'm not part of the nursery anymore.* Instead, she said, "Oui, Papa," and carried Hélène out of the room.

"You must be quiet at the table, Anne. You know that," she scolded the five-year-old as they walked together down the hall. "I remember how hard it is," Marie told her. She thought about how long the meals had seemed before she was allowed to speak at the table. "When we get back to the nursery, you can play and run in the garden."

I could use a wild run, too, she thought. Papa had been as cranky as the little girls since he'd gotten back from Versailles. Maman was tense, too.

"Thank you, Marie," the nursemaid said. Marie looked around the nursery once before she left. It was so small! Thérèse knocked over a chair, and Anne started to cry.

"Do you remember being the only child?" Nurse asked. Marie nodded. She handed the sobbing Hélène to Nurse. "It is very different here now," she said. "Too noisy."

Marie hurried back to the dining room. *I don't want a house full of babies,* she thought. The café would seem quiet today, no matter how many arguments began at the tables. At least with grown-ups, there were no tears, she thought.

The breakfast dishes had been cleared when Marie got back to the dining room. Maman, Papa, and Monsieur Williams were drinking coffee. They looked startled when she entered. "Oh, Marie," Maman said quickly. "Would you see that the café is ready to open, please?"

"But," Marie began. When she saw the look on her mother's face, she decided not to argue. What was happening? Marie wandered into the quiet front room. The tables were in place, of course. The maids had seen to that last night. She straightened a tablecloth that was already straight, and piled the napkins more neatly. Marie looked around. There was nothing left to do.

She wandered to the front door and peeked out at a gray morning. There seemed to be a lot of people on the street. It wasn't the usual crowd of merchants and businessmen, either. No children were outdoors playing. None of the nuns from the nearby convent was strolling by. Most of these people were men—students and workers. They were all heading past the café's closed doors toward the pastry shop.

Marie stepped outside. "Bonjour, Henri!" she called to a passing student.

"Ave!" Henri worked his way through the crowd to her side. "Have you seen Joelle?" he asked.

"Non. Is something wrong?"

"The king."

"Something has happened to the king?" Marie's heart pounded as if she'd been dancing a wild jig.

He shook his head. "King Louis *is* the problem," he said. "He's the reason there's no flour in all of Paris. The king won't let farmers bring grain here from other parts of France. It is such a mistake."

A king make a mistake? It couldn't be. Kings always knew best, didn't they? Marie thought hard as she watched the crowds pass. Henri was wrong, she decided. "Where is everyone going?" she asked him.

"They're looking for flour. They've broken into bakeries and storehouses all over this quarter of town."

"But that's wrong!" Marie said. Henri shrugged and joined the crowd.

"Bonjour, Marie." It was Prudence. She stood beside Marie, looking at all the people. "Is there a street fair today?"

"Non. Henri says they are all looking for flour for their families."

A large man pushed past them. "Let's go inside, Marie," Prudence suggested. Marie locked the door behind them. "I don't like the look of that crowd," Prudence said. "Joelle would be much safer at your house today than at her pastry shop."

"Henri said they've already broken into some bakeries."

"Then we haven't a moment to lose! Is there another way to get to Joelle?"

"There is a secret passageway to a side door," Marie said. "But nobody uses it."

"So much the better," Prudence said. "Let's hurry."

Near a corner in the café, Marie opened a closet. "This way," she said, rushing through a door in the back of the closet. Beyond was a passage that led to a back hall stairway. "Follow me," she called, pushing open a door hidden amid the trees in the garden behind the house.

"Marie, why is this here?" Prudence asked, panting.

"All buildings have secret passageways," Marie explained as she pushed on a colored brick in the garden wall. "I suspect I don't even know all of them in our house. Don't American homes have them?"

Prudence shook her head. "Non." Part of the wall swung open, and they could hear the sound of breaking glass from beyond.

"Joelle!" Marie shouted, squeezing through and running to Joelle's back door. "It's me, it's me," she called, pounding on the door. At last the door opened. "Oh, thank Heavens you are safe!" Marie hugged her friend.

"Follow us," Prudence said. "You come, too, Madame Du Pont." They hurried back through the passages into the café. "Let's get away from the windows," Prudence suggested, leading them into the dining room.

Maman looked at their faces. "What has happened?" she asked.

Papa pulled a chair out so Joelle's maman could sit down as Marie explained everything.

"Then it has begun," Madame Du Pont said, slowly shaking her head.

"Oh, Papa!" Marie cried. "Does this mean a revolution is starting today? Prudence still has to paint Paris, and I'm going to the Opéra the day after tomorrow, and . . ." She stopped, thinking how silly she sounded.

"I don't know what to tell you, ma chérie," Papa said. His voice was very sad.

"In Boston," Monsieur Williams said, "in the Commonwealth of Massachusetts, some men got so angry over King George's taxes that they stole tea right off a boat and dumped it into the harbor. They called it the *Boston Tea Party* to make fun of it. Many of us thought war would start that very week."

"Did it?" Marie asked. She held her breath.

"Non," Prudence told her, "and that was more than two years ago."

"Thank goodness," Maman sighed in relief.

"But it is certain that the real fighting will start soon," Monsieur Williams said. Madame Du Pont buried her head in her hands and began to weep.

"Papa," Joelle called. "Papa? Are you all right?" The La Marches followed her carefully through the broken glass and drifts of flour on the shop floor. Counters had been overturned, signs torn from the walls, and snarls of string and wrapping paper thrown to the floor. Huge metal mixing bowls were tossed about like child's toys. The sharp smell of yeast hung in the air, and a money box lay empty by the door.

Madame Du Pont hurried into the back room. "Oh, Mon Dieu!" they heard her curse. Papa rushed to help.

"Wait," Maman ordered the girls. She kept one hand firmly on Joelle's shoulder and another on Marie's. "Papa and Madame Du Pont can handle things." Joelle wiggled free and darted toward the back room. Before Marie could join her, Monsieur Du Pont limped out.

"I am safe," he told them quickly. "Just stiff from being tied." He hugged his daughter.

"They didn't hurt you, Papa?" Joelle asked.

"Non, ma chérie." He kissed the top of her head. "Their fight was not with me." Marie knew he meant that the fight was with the king himself. It made her feel sick to her stomach. King Louis XVI was, well, the king. And no one could question a king's power. She swallowed hard.

"I'll help clean the mess up," she offered. It would feel good to move around, to sweep buckets of flour and trampled croissants from the floor, and to hurl broken glass into a trash barrel. She looked out through the broken front window at the gray day. Suddenly a policeman was staring back at her.

"Who did this?" he demanded. Joelle's papa limped forward. "Do you know the names of any of your attackers?" the policeman repeated.

Henri was there, Marie thought. And she'd seen a dozen more of the students who ate at the café every day. *Take care,* she reminded herself, and decided to say nothing. The policeman got only shrugged shoulders from everyone in answer to his questions. "Very well," he said. "I see." He turned to go. "I shall find others with better memories." He snapped an angry salute to them all before he left.

The men began the heavy cleanup work while Marie's maman and Madame Du Pont swept. Joelle gathered pots and pans. Marie picked up the money box and searched for any coins the mob had missed in the floury mess. There wasn't even one *sou* left for the Du Ponts.❖

THE MARIONETTE

"Let's see if the puppet theater is open," Marie suggested to Joelle. The warm spring morning was too lovely to spend indoors.

Joelle's face brightened. "Remember how we always watched them together when we were little girls, Marie? That was before our shop was robbed. . . ." Her face fell again.

"We could see if Prudence would like to come with us," Marie added quickly. "She's probably never seen a marionette." Joelle sighed and straightened her cap.

The three girls ran the last block to the puppet theater. "Oh, non!" Marie cried as they turned the corner. "Closed," she read the sign aloud. "Next show this afternoon."

"And I shall have to be home to help by

then," Joelle said. "Nothing is going right. Oh, what a terrible day!" She sat on an empty bench and buried her chin into her hand.

"What is so special about marionettes?" Prudence asked.

Marie could tell she was trying to help. "They are wooden, with hinges where we have joints," she explained, pointing at the puppets on the poster. "Strings move them, almost as if they were alive."

"Aren't they stiff?"

"Non." Marie tried to think how she could explain. "I'll show you," she said. She walked to a grassy spot by Joelle's bench and swung a leg, stiff but free at the same time. "The string goes to the knee, here," she pointed. "When the puppeteer pulls the string, the leg lifts." She pulled up on an imaginary thread, and her knee jerked upward. Prudence laughed out loud, and Joelle looked up. "The foot flops around"— Marie shook a loose foot— "but when the leg goes down"— she let the leg fall— "the foot slaps down just right."

"What about the arms?" Prudence asked.

"They have strings tied to their elbows"— Marie raised her elbows high and let her hands swing down— "and more strings at the hands."

Now she lifted her hands and let her elbows swing. She waved at Joelle with one hand, then pretended to clap, bringing her stiff hands together in front of her in great sweeping motions.

Now Joelle laughed. "Show Prudence how they dance," she said.

Marie grinned for a minute, then made her face stiff as if it were painted. There would be strings here, and here, and there, she reminded herself. And she couldn't bend here. Or there. Everywhere Madame always had told her to make graceful curves, a marionette had sharp angles. This was going to be fun! She kept her eyes straight ahead and imagined one string pulling her head up, and another hooked through the top of her skirt to her *derrière*. Her arms swung to the sides, and she suddenly dropped forward at the waist in a puppet curtsy.

"Bravo!" Joelle said. Marie supposed that was her clapping, too, but she wouldn't let herself look. Prudence laughed aloud, and Marie heard a little child giggling. She felt foolish with her derrière higher than her head, but, for a mari-onette, it was just right.

So was the dance that followed, all angles and

slapping feet, sweeping turns and giant steps.
The more she danced, the more laughter followed
her moves. She could hear children laughing now,
and men, little old ladies, and boys, too.
Marie-the-marionette loved the beautiful, happy

sound that
accompanied her
dance. She tried
new moves and
sillier still, until,
breathless, she
flopped over
into a grand
marionette curtsy.

"Bravo!"
people cried. "Bravo!" Laughter filled the street.

"Marie? Marie!" It took a minute to realize
that Prudence wanted her to answer, and another
moment to remember how.

"Oui?" she finally said, moving only her lips.

"What happens if the strings are cut?"

Marie-the-marionette jerked upward and
stood still for a moment, one arm outstretched
and the other over her head as if to turn. If no
other power controlled her, she thought, she
would fall to the ground like a rag doll. And then

the show—and all the beautiful laughter—
would be over. She didn't want it to stop. What if
Marie-the-marionette had a mind of its own?

She crumpled suddenly onto the grass. One at
a time she made her parts move on their own.
First a finger twitched. Then a shoulder shrugged.
An elbow pulled her arm upward until she was
sitting. Her head nodded in time to music only
she could follow and then to the laughter that all
could hear.

She ended in control of her whole body, with
one deep and thoroughly graceful curtsy and then
another. Finally Marie let her eyes come into
focus. *Mon Dieu!* she thought suddenly. I played
the puppet in front of all these people?

A dozen little children sat on the grass. Their
parents stood near them, clapping. A cluster of
nuns, a policeman, and even a street merchant
with her basket full of eggs had stopped to watch.
A row of university students stood in their long
black gowns, trying not to look too interested.
There was a flash of yellow from behind them. As
Marie watched, a fine lady in a lace-covered dress
stepped into sight. Her hair was piled high with
curls, powdered snowy white, then topped with
ribbons and fresh flowers. Marie gasped. It was

the same aristocrat who had watched her dance with the Harlequin! The great lady's green eyes looked friendly, and she, too, was clapping.

Marie pictured herself, flopping over with her derrière pointed to the sky, mocking a curtsy to this lady. To them all. How foolish she must have looked! Marie's face reddened, and she turned and ran from the green.

"Marie! Wait, Marie!" It was Prudence and Joelle. Marie stopped. Joelle caught up with her and threw her arms around Marie.

"Do you know how happy you make people?" Prudence asked. Neither she nor Joelle could seem to stop grinning.

"Or how rich you could be?" Joelle opened her apron pocket and showed Marie dozens and dozens of copper coins. "So many sous!" she said. "I told people, non, that you would not want money, but they had to thank you somehow."

"What shall I do with all of it?" Marie asked. "I can't keep it." She had a sudden picture of the empty money box at the pastry shop and started grinning as gaily as her friends.❖

THE BRIDGE

"Could you take me to paint a bridge today, Marie?" Prudence asked. Marie looked at Maman. "My papa says there are lots of interesting people by a bridge," Prudence explained to Madame La Marche. "That would give my painting even more color."

"There are, indeed, many people crossing to the city island. Will you be careful?" Maman asked.

"Of course, Madame."

"Perhaps you should take Joelle, too, so there are more of you." Maman still looked doubtful.

"That is a wonderful idea, Maman," Marie gushed. "Joelle is still sad about her store. It would be good for her. We could pack a meal and picnic by the river, non?"

"You must promise to be back long before

dark," Maman said. Marie and Prudence nodded to her and headed to the pastry shop.

"What have you planned for the picnic?" Joelle asked when they found her. "Maman saved three éclairs from yesterday. I know she would want you to have them."

"Cook packed crusty rolls and mayonnaise to spread on them," Marie said.

"What's mayonnaise?" Prudence asked.

"It is a wonderful new sauce. There's nothing in it but eggs and oil, vinegar and spices, but it is velvety and thick and rich," Joelle said. "Wait until you taste it!"

"I'm hungry already," Prudence said, then added, "I think." All three laughed then headed toward the bridge. The farther they walked, the more people crowded the street. Men in white wigs rode past on horseback, and footmen raced ahead of carriages, shouting, "Make way! Make way!"

"This is perfect," Prudence said as the bridge came into view. Vendors had set up booths against the wall. Customers were arguing over the prices of meat or cheese. Others shopped for scarves or jewelry, gloves or medicine. "I could paint here for days!"

"Non, you can't," Marie said with a smile. "We have to be home in a few hours."

"Oh, look!" Prudence cried. "A bookseller! I love books, don't you?" She led the way to the street vendor's booth.

"Oui." Marie followed along and reached for a leather-covered volume. "Books about dance are the best of all, of course. But I love stories that make me think about other people and other times, too."

"Give me a rainy afternoon, a warm blanket, and an art book, and I'm happy." Prudence smiled. "Or a good history book. What about you, Joelle?"

"I can't read," Joelle said. She picked up bright-colored silk scarves from the next booth.

"They didn't teach you to read in school?"

"Marie reads only because her parents taught her," Joelle said. "Neither of us has been to school, but we're both going this fall."

"We are?" Marie asked.

"I heard your maman talking to mine," Joelle said. "We're both going to study at the convent of Sainte-Geneviève's." Marie's whole body froze, her hand resting on a dance book. *Non!* her mind screamed. *Not yet! I haven't even begun to dance.*

"Are you both going to be nuns?"

"Oh, non," Joelle giggled. "Girls just go to convent school so they can learn enough Latin to understand Mass at church. We'll sing and do needlepoint and geography. . . ." Joelle held a flowered scarf into the sunlight.

"Do they teach dance at convent schools?" Prudence asked.

"Oh, non. We'll stay for a few years until our papas find husbands for us. Then we'll marry." Joelle wrapped the scarf around her shoulders. "I can't wait."

"Are you sure you heard them right?" Marie asked in a choked whisper.

"Oh, yes. It will be such fun to be there with you and the other girls and all the nuns!"

"Oh, Marie," Prudence put her hand on Marie's. "I'm so sorry." Her voice was full of understanding. "Perhaps Joelle heard wrong?"

Marie shook her head. "That is what most girls do," she said. Now her voice just sounded tired. *Not me!* the argument raged in her head.

Not yet! She stretched her neck tall and pushed her shoulders down, the way Gabrielle had taught her, and turned to face Joelle and Prudence. "Somehow," she promised them, "I am going to dance. I'll find a way."

In silence, Marie helped Prudence set up her easel. "You must not let any chance go by," the American girl told her, "but you must not let a friendship go by, either." Marie thought about what she'd said to Joelle, and gasped. She looked around quickly. Her friend was sitting on a nearby bench, staring at the river.

"Oh, no!" Marie said and ran to her side. "Joelle, ma chérie, no matter what happens, we must always stay friends, non?"

"Oui," Joelle said. "I only wish we wanted the same things."

"C'est la vie," Marie said.

"But *I'm* the one who always says that!" Joelle said, and both girls started to laugh. "Let's share the picnic now." Joelle opened the basket and handed Marie a chocolate éclair. "Friends always," she said, and bit into her pastry.

"Friends," Marie said, and let herself nibble at the sweet pastry.

"Pardon me, Mademoiselle," a small voice said

at her elbow. It was a little girl, not much older than Anne, but so skinny that she looked sick. She was dressed in rags and held the hand of a still smaller child. Both little faces were full of sadness. "Can you spare a little for my sister, here? She is so hungry." The girls were barefoot and spattered with Paris street mud.

"Did either of you have breakfast?" Joelle asked gently.

"Non, nor any supper last night." Marie and Joelle looked at each other for only a moment before they handed their éclairs to the girls.

"Where are your parents?"

"Maman has gone to the priest to ask for help. Papa is begging the streets for a sou so we can have dinner. Please, do you have more?" The little girl was staring at the basket. Her dirty hands grabbed and pulled at her rags. Marie suddenly pictured the yellow dress on the green-eyed aristocrat. How many sous had that dress cost? she wondered. And how many dresses did that woman have? "Take the whole basket," she said, pushing it at the beggar girl. "I only wish we had more."

"Mon Dieu," Joelle said as the little girls raced across the street to share the picnic with three other beggar children. More raggedy-dressed children ran to join them.

"Perhaps a king *can* make a mistake," Marie said slowly. She helped Prudence fold her easel, and they headed home.

On the long walk, she kept remembering the little girls' sad, sad faces. "I can make them happy," she said suddenly.

"What?" Joelle and Prudence turned to look at her.

"My dancing makes people happy. I saw it myself." Marie was thinking fast now. "And perhaps I could earn sous for those poor children's suppers, too."❖

MARIE'S BALLET

The opera house was crowded and noisy as Monsieur Williams led Prudence, Joelle, and Marie to their seats. "Madame Gabrielle wishes you to join her backstage after the performance," Prudence's papa said. "She said she has a surprise for you."

Marie could hardly sit still as the huge curtains opened. It was like magic, she thought. Lanterns along the edge of the stage flickered as they lit the scenery. One singer came out, then another. They sang of love and sorrow. A man strutted onstage, dressed as a fool. He sang like one, too, and the audience laughed loudly. His face didn't change at the sound of their laughter, or the applause that followed, but Marie knew the joy he was feeling.

As she watched, a story unfolded onstage. The

actors spoke and mimed and sang and never forgot who they were pretending to be. "They're like Prudence," Marie whispered to Joelle. "When she is painting, she forgets who she is."

"Non, they're like Marie," Joelle whispered back, "who really became a marionette." Marie smiled in the darkness. Around them people talked and laughed. A dog began barking from the royal box seats above them, and many people hissed, "Hush!" Beside them a man popped open a bottle of champagne.

"Is it always this noisy at the Opéra?" Prudence whispered.

Marie shrugged. "It sounds like this at Mass in the cathedrals," she answered.

Finally the dancers walked into view. Their skirts were just as short as Madame had said, Marie thought, and they looked lovely. If their feather-topped wigs were stiff or their makeup thick, it didn't show from the audience. When they started to dance, Marie sat up in her seat. They were doing the same steps that Gabrielle had taught her!

It was so much more beautiful with live musicians playing, and lanterns and scenery—but it was her own dance. Marie swayed along in the darkness. *I could do that,* she told herself as the dog finally stopped barking. The music filled Marie's mind, she could feel every step and turn in her muscles, and she began to imagine that she was dancing onstage. Dancers on both sides of her dipped and swayed in time, and her steps flowed perfectly. Suddenly the music stopped. Marie blinked and looked around. The audience was applauding wildly. The dancers curtsied, and the curtain came down.

"Hurry, Marie. Down here!" It was Gabrielle, waving to her from the front of the theater. As the others headed toward the lobby, Marie made her way down to the stage. "Here is your surprise," Gabrielle said. She held a tall white wig out toward Marie. Stiff feathers topped the hairpiece—feathers that matched the ballet dancers' costumes. Marie did not dare to think what it meant.

"Hurry now," Gabrielle said. "We barely have time before the opera house closes for the night. I wish to introduce you to an old friend of mine." She laced Marie tightly into a stage costume and led her out into the lobby.

"Oh, Marie, you look lovely," Prudence said. She turned to Gabrielle. "Madame, is there any chance I might try on a dance costume?"

"Non," Gabrielle said firmly. "This is only for Marie."

"Look. How beautiful!" Joelle cried. Marie followed her gaze to the huge curving staircase. "Have you ever seen so many bows and roses and braids and ribbons and tassels?" Gabrielle's friend stood posed on the top stair, her servants and ladies clustered beside her.

"All that lace!" Marie answered. "And look at her hairstyle. That's a perfect model ship on top. With sails." The lady glided down the stairs. A little dog followed her on a thin gold ribbon, barking at all the people in their wigs and satins.

"That's the lady from the park," Joelle whispered.

The aristocrat's tiny footsteps tapped across the marble floor toward the girls. "Mademoiselle Marie La Marche?"

"Oui?" Marie whispered. What was this all about?

"You look enchanting in that costume. Now I would like to see you in the dance."

"What?" Marie gasped. "Here? You want me to dance now? In the lobby?"

"Gabrielle assures me that you do know the steps."

"But . . . ?" Marie looked at Gabrielle.

"You are like my own child," Madame said. "And you must dance." She hugged Marie. "I have told my old friend of your skill. The rest is up to you. I'm sure you know what to do."

And Marie did. She began to keep count in her head, then posed to start the dance Gabrielle had taught her, the steps she'd imagined dancing with the other ballerinas. Marie closed her eyes and pictured the stage, the scenery, and the lights. In her mind, she heard the music start.

When she opened her eyes, the empty white marble of the lobby floor was gone. There was only the dance and the stage she imagined around her. Marie stepped and swayed, turned and paused with the other dancers she could almost see on either side. She danced higher and brighter than she ever had before, each step as close to perfect as she could make it.

This is my chance, Marie chanted in time to the music in her head. *My chance.* She kept her eyes focused on Gabrielle as she twirled the last wild pirouette. "Thank you, Madame," she whispered, bringing the dance to a graceful close. In her mind, applause washed over her, and Marie dropped into a full court curtsy. The audience

began yelling, "Bravo!" and Marie curtsied yet again.

"I am very impressed," Gabrielle's friend said, and suddenly Marie realized she was not onstage. There was no orchestra. No scenery. The audience was simply her friends, a few strangers and servants, and the woman from the royal box. "Gabrielle tells me," she was saying, "that you are in need of a sponsor for training and placement, non? You have certainly proven yourself today. May I help you?"

Marie could not speak. *Take care with your words,* she reminded herself. Her mind raced. *What would Maman say? Maman is sending me away soon anyway.* Marie's hands began to tremble.

"Make up your mind, little one," the woman said. The dog pulled at its leash.

Marie took a great breath and held her hands together to steady them.

She looked at Prudence, and then at Joelle.

"Oui, Madame," she told the great lady at last. "I am yours." ❖

JOURNEY TO PARIS, 1775

In 1775, Paris was the biggest city in all Europe. That meant it was the biggest city in all of the world. Fashion and learning, art and literature flowed from Paris to all of France and to the French colonies everywhere.

The French court had just celebrated the crowning of a new king, Louis XVI, and his beautiful young queen, Marie Antoinette. Not all of the people could celebrate, though. Taxes to the royal court and the churches were so high that most people were poor. Many were so poor that they went hungry.

Perspective view of Paris in the eighteenth century

Few minded giving
money to the
Catholic Church.
It ran schools
and hospitals
and fed the
poorest. And it
gave everyone
magnificent cathedrals
where they could worship

King Louis XVI and Queen Marie Antoinette

and feel—at least for a time—as if they owned
part of something very rich.

People felt different about the court, however.
All of the nobles had moved outside of Paris to a
special royal city, Versailles, where they spent the
people's tax money foolishly. While the French
people struggled to feed their children, the queen
bought diamonds to decorate her walls, gold
bowls for her dogs, and a whole new palace to use
as her own private playhouse.

People began to complain. They had heard
about the coming American revolution. Writers
told them about a strange new idea: equality.
People struggled with the idea that a king or
queen might really be no better a person than a
farmer or a pastry cook. Some could understand.

The Public Scribe

A few even began to believe it.

Paris was—and still is—a city of talkers. People gathered in the streets, in fancy dining rooms, and in small cafés to discuss the new ideas.

A French revolution was already brewing in 1775. Many Frenchmen went to the colonies and fought with the Americans against England. They came back home to France, convinced that revolution—and equality—would work there, too. The actual fighting did not start in Paris for fourteen more years, but a feeling of change was already in the air.

Ballet was changing, too. In 1775, ballerinas danced alongside singers to make the Opéra prettier. They wore regular street shoes, tall white wigs, and long dresses. A very few people were trying a new kind of dance—a ballet where the dance itself told the story. In these ballets, there was no speaking or singing, just beautiful music and pure dance. The leaps and jumps and steps grew far more difficult. To show off these new movements, dancers began to wear lighter, shorter costumes. Skirts rose above the ankles, to the knees, then above to become stiff tutus.

Talented young ballerinas began to dance the more difficult steps on their tiptoes. Then they made special shoes that stiffened their feet so they could dance on the very points of their toes. This all was a revolution in the dance. It was as hard for people to accept as was the idea of equality.

Once French people accepted the idea that all people were created equal, change came swiftly. The royal family was killed and, within a few years, France became a democracy.

Ballet changed swiftly, too, into the beautiful art form we know today.

Sometimes change is violent. Sometimes it is frightening. It can be exciting, and wonderful, and challenging, too, but it is never easy. Young people, students, and fresh new thinkers help to bring the change to the world. They did in 1775, and they still do today. ❖

KATHLEEN V. KUDLINSKI studied

 ballet as a little girl and now writes historical fiction, science books, and biographies for children, as well as a newspaper nature column. The mother of two children, she lives in Connecticut.

LYN DURHAM is a native of California and a graduate of the University of California at Berkeley. In addition to book illustration, Lyn enjoys painting large scale watercolors and full figure stained glass windows, usually with mythic or celestial subject matter. She lives in Fairfield, Iowa, with her husband, Steve Jacomini, and her daughter, Athena.

Juliet *Circa 1339*

Marie *Circa 177*

Kai *Circa 1440*

Shannon *Circa 188*

Enter a whole new world of friendships and exciting adventures!

Share the adventures of the young women of Girlhood Journeys™ with beautifully detailed dolls and fine quality books. Authentically costumed, each doll is based on the enchanting character from the pages of the fascinating book that accompanies her.

- Join our collectors club and share the fun with other girls who love Girlhood Journeys.
- Enter the special Girlhood Journeys essay contest.
- For more information call 1-800-553-4886.

Ertl Collectibles
L I M I T E D

Actual size of doll is 14".

GET READY TO GO ON A JOURNEY!

Join our Collectors' Club and share the fun with other girls who love Girlhood Journeys.

We've created the Girlhood Journeys Collectors' Club especially for girls like you—
bright and full of fun, and always ready to travel.

Read about it...in your free issue of *Girlhood Journals*, the newsletter that features interesting articles about *Girlhood Journeys* writers and artists, photos and stories from around the world, and excerpts from forthcoming books.

Wear it...on your hat, jacket, or backpack. You will be in fashion with a *Girlhood Journeys* pin.

Write it down...in your *Girlhood Journeys* Journal. You can create your own stories and characters or just jot down notes and ideas. We even give you a *Girlhood Journeys* pen!

Hang it...on your wall or place it on your desk. We're talking about a beautiful, signed, full-color illustration created especially for Girlhood Journeys Collectors' Club members.

Okay so how do I join? Membership is available with your purchase of a *Girlhood Journeys* doll. Simply look for the membership application form and information inside your *Girlhood Journeys* doll package.

YOU COULD WIN A *GIRLHOOD JOURNEYS* TRIP AND CHOOSE YOUR FAVORITE ADVENTURE!
Other great prizes too! See official rules below for complete details.

- Explore Kai's world on an African safari adventure.
- See the streets of Paris where Marie lived and danced on a special Paris holiday.
- Tour the castles and kingdoms of Juliet's time on a trip to London and the English countryside.

Or

- Ride the cable cars in San Francisco and visit Chinatown and Victorian sites where Shannon and her friends once played.

HOW TO ENTER: Write your own *Girlhood Journeys* adventure story about your favorite *Girlhood Journeys* doll. The story should be no longer than 500 words. Let your imagination run wild! The winner gets to choose the trip of her choice and have her story published in the *Girlhood Journals* newsletter.

OFFICIAL RULES – No Purchase Necessary

1. HOW TO ENTER: To enter the *Girlhood Journeys Writing Contest*, type or print on 8½"x 11" paper your name, address, age, daytime phone number (with area code) and your original 500 word or less essay written about an adventure taken by you and your favorite *Girlhood Journeys* doll. Mail your entry to: Girlhood Journeys Writing Contest, P.O. Box 8947, St. Louis, MO 63101. All entries must be received by December 31, 1997. The Ertl Company, Inc., is not responsible for late, lost, damaged, misdirected or postage-due mail. Illegible or incomplete entries will be disqualified. Only one entry per entrant. Entries must be original and not previously published in any medium. All entries become the property of The Ertl Company, Inc., and will not be returned. Winner must sign a release signing all rights to The Ertl Company, Inc.

2. JUDGING: The winners will be selected by an independent judging panel, whose decisions are final on all matters related to this contest, on or about January 31, 1998. Winners will be selected based on originality/creativity, writing skill, and appropriateness, in equal value. Only one prize per household or family. All prizes will be awarded.

3. NOTIFICATION: The Grand Prize winner will be notified by mail on or about February 18, 1998. Prize will be awarded in name of winner's parent or guardian who will be required to sign and return an affidavit of eligibility and liability and publicity release within 14 days of notification. Grand prize winner's travel companion must also sign a publicity/liability release and return it within the same time period. Travel companion must be 18 years or over or traveling with a parent or guardian. In the event of noncompliance within this time period, prize will be forfeited and an alternate winner will be selected. Any prize notification or prize returned to the sponsor or its agencies as undeliverable will result in disqualification and the awarding of that prize to an alternate winner. Acceptance of prize offered constitutes permission to use winner's name, biographical information and/or likeness for purposes of advertising and promotion without notice or further compensation as permitted by law.

4. ELIGIBILITY: Contest is open to residents of the United Sates who are 6-13 years of age. Employees and the immediate families of employees of The Ertl Company, Inc., its affiliates, subsidiaries, advertising and promotion agencies, and all retail licensees are ineligible. This contest is void where prohibited by law, and is subject to federal, state, and local regulations. Taxes on prizes, if any, are the responsibility of individual winners. By participating in this contest, participants agree to be bound by all Official Rules of this contest.

5. PRIZE DETAILS: Grand Prize (1): Trip for winner and one (1) guest to ONE of the following destinations: Trip Choice One • Paris, Chateaux and Countryside Holiday (9 nights); Trip Choice Two • African Safari Adventure (12 nights); Trip Choice Three • London and English Countryside (9 nights); Trip Choice Four • Victorian San Francisco (6 nights). Each trip for two (2) includes round-trip coach airfare (to/from the gateway city nearest the winner's home), double-occupancy accommodations, and a guided tour or safari. Travel must be taken by February 18, 1999. Estimated retail value of each trip for 2: $2,800.00–$9,270.00 based on destination selected and departure city. Meals, gratuities, and all other expenses not specified herein are winner's responsibility. First Prize (4): Gift set of the entire *Girlhood Journeys* book series published by Simon & Schuster. Estimated retail value: $23.95 each. Total estimated retail value of all prizes: $2,895.80–$9,365.80. Winners may not substitute or transfer prizes but sponsor reserves the right to substitute prizes with prizes of equal or greater value, if advertised prize becomes unavailable.

6. WINNERS' LIST: For a winners' list, send a self-addressed, stamped envelope by March 1, 1998 to: Girlhood Journeys Writing Contest Winners, P.O. Box 8980, St. Louis, MO 63101.